Jack the Bum and the Halloween Handout

by JANET SCHULMAN
pictures by JAMES STEVENSON

Greenwillow
Read-alone

GREENWILLOW BOOKS
A Division of William Morrow
& Company, Inc. | New York

In cooperation with the
U.S. Committee for UNICEF

Educ.
JF
Sch

Color separations by Harriet Sherman

Library of Congress Cataloging in Publication Data
Schulman, Janet. Jack the bum and the Halloween handout.
Summary: Jack the bum spends Halloween trying to get money for something to eat. But when he wins a prize for the best costume, he donates it to UNICEF [1. Halloween—Fiction. 2. United Nations. Children's Fund—Fiction] I. Stevenson, James, (date). II. Title. PZ7.S3866Jac   [E]   76-11032   ISBN 0-688-80057-2   ISBN 0-688-84057-4 lib. bdg.

To N. S., with love and laughs,

from J. S.

Jack pulled his hat down
over his ears.
"Brrr. It is cold," he said.
Grrr went his stomach.
"Quiet down there," said Jack.
"I sure would like
a cup of hot coffee."

He looked in his right pocket.

He found two buttons.

But no money.

He looked in his left pocket.

He found a big hole.

"Tonight is Halloween.
This is a good night to beg,"
said Jack.
Just then a big man
got out of a taxicab.

"Mister, can you spare me
some money for a cup of coffee?"
asked Jack.

"I only give money
to UNICEF on Halloween,"
the man said.
"Who is UNICEF?"
asked Jack.
"UNICEF is not a person.
It is a worthy cause,"
said the man.
"I am a worthy cause,"
said Jack.
"No. You are a bum,"
said the man.

Jack walked down the street.

There were many children

on the street.

They were dressed

in funny costumes

and scary costumes.

Each had a big full bag.
"These kids know
how to beg.
I will ask them
how to do it,"
said Jack.

"It is easy,"

said a little ghost to Jack.

"You ring a doorbell

and when someone opens the door,

you say:

    " 'Trick or treat,

    Smell my feet.

    Give me something

    Good to eat.' "

The children laughed.

"That sounds easy," said Jack.

He walked up to a house.

He rang the doorbell.

A woman opened the door.

Jack pushed his foot

into her face and said:

"Trick or treat,

Smell my feet.

Give me something

Good to eat."

She slammed the door in his face.

"I should have washed my socks,"

said Jack. "The next time

I will just say trick or treat."

Jack rang the next doorbell.

A man answered.

"What a clever costume you have!

We have had three witches,

four ghosts,

two clowns,

one Frankenstein,

 and a lot of

fairy princesses.

But you are our first bum tonight,"
the man said.

"Trick or treat," said Jack.

The man gave him a candy bar.

"I do not want candy," said Jack.

"I want money."

"Oh," said the man.

"Have you collected a lot already?"

"Certainly not," said Jack.

"Why do you think

I am asking you?"

"I do not believe that you are

collecting money for UNICEF,"

the man said.

And he slammed the door.

"UNICEF must be the magic word,"

said Jack.

He rang the next doorbell.

A woman opened the door.

"UNICEF or else!" said Jack.

The woman looked at Jack.

She looked at his big toes.

She looked at his shaggy beard.

"Aren't you a little old

for this sort of thing?" she asked.

And she slammed the door.

"I do not understand
what I am doing wrong,"
said Jack. "Maybe they want
a little entertainment
before they hand out money.
I will sing them a song
and do a little dance."

Jack saw a dark alley.
"This is a good place
to work on my song and dance.
No one will see me
or hear me," he said.
But alley cats saw him.
And alley cats heard him.

They did not like his singing.

"Yeowlll," went one cat.

Then all the cats began yeowling.

Jack sang louder and louder:

> "I wanna be loved by you,
>
> Just you,
>
> And nobody else but you,
>
> I wanna be loved.
>
> Boop boop a-doo."

Jack danced faster and faster.

He bumped into a garbage can.

CRASH! BANG!

A light went on in a window.
A bucket of water
came flying out of the window.
CRASH! SPLASH!

Jack was very wet.

He ran out of the alley.

"This is not a friendly place,"

said Jack.

Now the street
was full of children
in Halloween costumes.
Jack watched them.
They all were going
into a big building
with a tall fence around it.

"Whoever owns that house
must be very rich,"
said Jack.
He followed the children
up the steps.

They did not ring the doorbell.

They opened the door

and walked right in.

"Whoever owns this house

must be very friendly too,"

said Jack.

The children went into a big room.

Jack heard music.

"Good. They like music here.

I can do my song and dance.

Then they will give me money,"

said Jack.

It was a very big room
with a shiny wooden floor
and no furniture.
At both ends of the room
there was a hoop
hanging high on the wall.
"This is the funniest living room
that I have ever seen,"
said Jack.
He stood in a corner
and watched the children.
First they handed a small box
to a man.

Then they sat on the floor
or played tag
or tried to scare each other.
It was very noisy.

Suddenly the music stopped.

A man walked to the middle

of the floor.

"Attention, please," he shouted.

"We are ready to start

our Halloween party,

but first I have some good news.

We have counted all the nickels
and dimes and quarters
in your UNICEF boxes.
They add up to more
than we have ever before
collected for UNICEF."
Everyone cheered.

"Does everyone know
what UNICEF does?"
the man asked.
"It helps bring schools and
health care and better houses
to families all over the world.
UNICEF helps people
to help themselves."

Jack opened his eyes wide.

Now he knew

what the magic word meant.

"Oh, dear," he said.
"I didn't know the money
    was to help children.
    I didn't mean
    to trick anyone.
    All I wanted
    was a cup of hot coffee."
He walked slowly
toward the door.

"Now we are ready
to give a prize
for the best costume,"
the man continued.

"The prize goes

to that tall boy near the door,

the one dressed like a bum."

Everyone turned

and looked at Jack.

Jack turned

and looked for the tall boy

dressed like a bum.

"Come here, young man,

and get your prize,"

said the man.

43

A woman smiled at Jack.
"Go on," she said,
and she took him
to the middle of the floor.
"Don't be shy," she said.

"But I am just a bum.

I don't deserve a prize,"

said Jack.

The woman smiled again.

"Yes, you do.

Your costume

is very clever.

You must have

worked hard on it.

It is so real."

The man gave Jack

his prize.

It was a five dollar bill!

"How can I make them
understand that I am not
a boy dressed like a bum?"
thought Jack.
Then he smiled.
"Don't you want to know
who I really am?
Here, pull off my beard
and mustache,"
said Jack to the man.
"Okay," said the man and
he grabbed at Jack's beard.

"OW!" said Jack.

"You didn't have to pull
so hard."

"Hey! You aren't a boy
dressed like a bum.
You are a real bum,"
the man said.

"That's what I've been trying
to tell you," shouted Jack.
The children laughed.
Then the man and the woman
and all the grownups laughed.
And so did Jack.

He looked at the five dollar bill.

"Can I keep my prize anyway?"

asked Jack.

"Well, I don't know . . . ,"

the man started to say.

"Because," Jack continued,

"I want to help poor children, too.

Here is five more dollars

to add to your UNICEF collection."

And he gave the money to the man.

Everyone cheered.

The man shook hands with Jack.

"Thank you," the man said.

"Now let's all celebrate

with cookies and cider,

and coffee for the grownups."

"Coffee! Did I hear someone

say coffee?" asked Jack.

"Sure. Help yourself.

Have as much as you want.

You are our guest of honor tonight.

You made our Halloween party

the best ever," the man said.

Jack drank one cup of coffee.

And another cup.

He ate a dozen cookies
and washed them down
with a third cup of coffee.

And then he felt so good

that he did his song and dance.

"I wanna be loved by you,

Just you,

And nobody else but you,

I wanna be loved.

Boop boop a-doo."

And everyone cheered for Jack.

JANET SCHULMAN was born in Pittsburgh, Pennsylvania, and was graduated from Antioch College in Yellow Springs, Ohio. She has been a copywriter, advertising manager, and for many years was marketing director for a major publisher of children's books in New York City.

JAMES STEVENSON is well known to readers of *The New Yorker* magazine as an artist, writer and reporter. He has a syndicated political comic strip and has written and illustrated many books for children and adults.